```
The wooly mammoth /
JUV 569.6 San                        28755
Sanford, William R.
        HAMBURG TOWNSHIP LIBRARY
```

D1786350

DISCARD

# GONE FOREVER

THE WOOLLY MAMMOTH

by William R. Sanford
and Carl R. Green

CRESTWOOD HOUSE
New York

LIBRARY OF CONGRESS CATALOGING IN PUBLICATION DATA

Sanford, William R. (William Reynolds), 1927-
The woolly mammoth / by William R. Sanford and Carl R. Green

p. cm. – (Gone forever)
Includes index.
SUMMARY: Describes what is known of this prehistoric ancestor of the elephant, based on the preserved remains of mammoth bodies.
1. Woolly mammoth–Juvenile literature. [1. Woolly mammoth. 2. Mammoths. 3. Mammals, Fossil 4. Prehistoric animals. 5. Paleontology.] I. Green, Carl R. II. Title. III. Series.
QE 882.P8S25   1989   569'.6–dc20   89-31575
ISBN 0-89686-456-1   CIP
                                                                                         AC

Photo Credits

DRK Photo: (Don & Pat Valenti) 11, 15, 35; (Stephen J. Krasemann) 5, 7, 20, 22; (Belinda Wright) 6; (Stanley Breeden) 18, 25
Photo Researchers, Inc.: 10, 32; (Tom McHugh) 27
Third Coast Stock Source: (J. P. Slater) 8, 44
George C. Page Museum of La Brea Discoveries: 9, 16
Frank Sloan: 13
Culver Pictures, Inc: 29, 30
FPG International: 38
Bettmann Archives, Inc.: 41

Cover illustrations by Kristi Schaeppi

Consultant: Professor Robert E. Sloan, Paleontologist
University of Minnesota

Copyright © 1989 by Crestwood House, Macmillan Publishing Company

All rights reserved. No part of this book may be reproduced or transmitted in any form or by any means, electronic or mechanical, including photocopying, recording, or by any information storage and retrieval system, without permission in writing from the Publisher.

Macmillan Publishing Company
866 Third Avenue
New York, NY 10022
Collier Macmillan Canada, Inc.

CRESTWOOD HOUSE

Produced by Carnival Enterprises

Printed in the United States of America

First Edition

10 9 8 7 6 5 4 3 2 1

Contents

Mammoths, Mastodons, and Elephants 4
The Mammoth's Family Tree 10
The Woolly Mammoth 14
The Mammoth's Trunk 17
A Hungry Giant 21
The Birth of a Woolly Mammoth 23
Did Stone Age People Hunt the Woolly Mammoth? 26
The Mystery of the Mammoth's Extinction 30
The Mystery of the Giant Bones 33
Mammoths in the Ice 36
The Creation of Fossils 39
Scientists Recreate a Woolly Mammoth 42
What Have We Learned? 45
For More Information 46
Glossary/Index 47-48

The woolly mammoth's habitat covered parts of Africa, Asia, North America, and Central America.

Mammoths, Mastodons, and Elephants

Imagine visiting a museum display called GIANTS OF THE PAST. You walk past the dinosaurs and come to the room of the giant mammals. There, side by side, stand some of

A life-size replica of the woolly mammoth greets visitors in this outdoor museum.

The Asiatic elephant is one of two species of elephants that are alive today.

history's largest warm-blooded land animals. Each one has a long *trunk*. All of them have *ivory* tusks. Some are almost hairless. Others have heavy coats of shaggy hair.

According to the name tags, the great beasts are called MAMMOTH, MASTODON, and ELEPHANT. Your first thought is, Those are all elephants!

A *naturalist* would disagree. Although the animals are similar, they are not the same. They vary in the structure of their teeth, the length and shape of their tusks, and in their body size. Let's see how each one fits into the picture.

At one time as many as 25 *species* of elephants lived on

Its huge ears and large size set the African elephant apart from its cousin, the Asiatic elephant.

the earth. Today only two species survive. These are the elephants you see in zoos and at the circus. The Asiatic elephant has the scientific name of *Elephas indicus*. African elephants are called *Loxodonta africana*. Both are true elephants, but African and Asiatic elephants cannot *interbreed*. You can tell them apart because Asiatic elephants are smaller, have much smaller ears, and have domed foreheads. The African elephants' huge ears are twice as big and they have flat foreheads.

At first glance it's easy to confuse the mastodon with the mammoth. After all, both have long trunks and curving

This mastodon skeleton is on display in the Milwaukee Public Museum in Wisconsin.

tusks. But mastodons are smaller. Smaller doesn't mean tiny, however. The American mastodon (*Mammut americanum*) stood nine feet tall at the shoulder. It weighed more than a modern elephant of the same height.

Mastodons lived in forests and woodlands, while mammoths lived on open grasslands. The mastodon's teeth were designed for crushing tree bark, leaves, and twigs. The word *mastodon* comes from two Greek words that describe the bumpy chewing surface of the animal's teeth. In addition, the mastodon's tusks were shorter and straighter than those of the mammoth. Like the mammoth, size alone

The imperial mammoth had longer tusks than the mastodon. This skeleton can be seen at the George Page Museum in Los Angeles, California.

wasn't enough to save the mastodon. These great elephant-like animals became extinct after human hunters invaded their *habitats*. A habitat is anywhere a species lives.

The mammoth is most like the modern elephant. At one time, scientists called it *Elephas primigenius,* or the "first-born elephant." Blood tests seemed to confirm the woolly mammoth is related to the Asiatic elephant. But closer study showed that the mammoth's bones, tusks, and teeth put it in a different *genus*. The mammoth has a different number of ribs. Its skull isn't shaped like an elephant's. As a result, the mammoth's scientific name was changed to

This painting of a herd of mastodons shows them near a forest, their natural habitat.

Mammuthus. This gave the woolly mammoth its official name, *Mammuthus primigenius.*

The woolly mammoth is a strange and impressive animal. How did it develop? A look at the mammoth's family tree tells the story.

The Mammoth's Family Tree

The woolly mammoth's earliest ancestors appeared on the earth during the age of the dinosaurs. The first mam-

The mammoth reached its full size about 20 million years ago. It was one of the largest warm-blooded animals in history.

mals were not like cold-blooded, egg-laying reptiles. The mammals were warm-blooded and gave birth to live young. Although they were no bigger than rats, these animals were quick and adaptable. Because they were warm-blooded, changes in the climate didn't affect them as much as it did the reptiles and dinosaurs. The dinosaurs died out about 65 million years ago. And the mammals were ready to take their place. As their numbers grew, many new species developed.

One possible forerunner of the mammoth lived about 40 million years ago. Moeritherium was about two feet tall. Its long head probably ended in a flexible snout. Scientists are not sure, because soft body parts like snouts and trunks don't make good *fossils*. The plant-eating Moeritherium lived in swamps and may have looked like a small hippopotamus.

Five million years later a more direct ancestor of the mammoth appeared. The first Paleomastodon was four feet tall. Two enlarged teeth, or tusks, jutted forward from its lower jaw. The animal probably used its tusks like a shovel to dig up the plants on which it fed. The Paleomastodon also had a flexible snout that was long enough to be called a trunk. It used its trunk to gather grasses and other plants because it could not reach the ground with its short, thick neck. The trunk was also good for squirting water and checking out strange objects.

Later, Paleomastodon reached seven feet in height. At the same time, even larger animals were developing. Food was plentiful, and greater size meant greater safety from *predators*. By 20 million years ago, Trilophodon had grown to the size of a modern elephant. This great beast had four tusks and a longer trunk than Paleomastodon. Because its jaws were shorter its trunk became more important.

The success of these elephantlike animals led to four major families of trunked mammals. These were the mastodons, mammoths, and the ancestors of today's Asiatic and African elephants. The oldest mammoths, called Archidiskodons, lived before the *ice ages* began, about a million years ago. One of them, the imperial mammoth, sometimes reached 14 feet in height. This giant weighed close to 20 tons. Except for Baluchiterium (a long-necked,

Large statues recreate mammoths and mastodons being trapped in the La Brea tar pits in Los Angeles.

hornless rhinoceros), it was the largest land mammal ever to walk the earth. A number of imperial mammoths died after being trapped in California's famous La Brea tar pits. The tar pits are located in Los Angeles, and the fossils are on display nearby at the George C. Page Museum.

Archidiskodon could not adapt to the changes that came with the ice ages. Mammoths that could survive in a cold climate took their places. In North America, the Columbian mammoth survived until about 10,000 years ago. In Europe, another hairy mammoth was probably the forerunner of the smaller woolly mammoth. The woolly mammoth appeared during the third ice age, some 300,000 years ago. With its heavy fur this great mammal did well in the ice-age cold. It became the most successful of all the mammoths.

The Woolly Mammoth

In English the word *mammoth* means something really large. A 40-story building is tall, but the tallest building in the world is mammoth! The animal that is now called mammoth was indeed gigantic.

The imperial mammoth truly deserved its name. These great beasts measured 14 feet high at the shoulder. The huge hump on their backs added another two or three feet to their heights. The body of the largest woolly mammoth ever found was only 11 feet tall. The average woolly mammoth was nine feet. That's about the size of today's Asiatic elephant. The imperial mammoth would have dwarfed the woolly mammoth.

The woolly mammoth's coat of shaggy fur made it look larger than it really was. The thick, two-layered coat helped the animal survive the intense cold of its habitat. The outer coat varied from brown to a rusty red in color. The long, coarse hair ranged in length from 4 inches on the legs to 18 inches on the back and sides. Under the mammoth's belly the shaggy hair sometimes hung almost to the ground. Underneath this coarse outer hair was a fine, woolly coat of one-inch fur. During each arctic summer the woolly mammoth shed its coat and grew a new one.

As animals grow larger they need bigger bones and muscles to support their weight. The woolly mammoth's body fit this rule of nature. The barrel-shaped body hung from a nearly rigid backbone and was supported by legs as thick as tree trunks. The sole of each foot was a round, elastic pad that cushioned each heavy step. Despite its size the mammoth could move with surprising speed.

The woolly mammoth's body was well adapted in other ways as well. It stored fat in two humps, probably as a reserve for times when food was hard to find. One small hump formed on top of the animal's head. The second, larger hump was located on the mammoth's broad back, over the front shoulders. The mammoth's ears and tail were

Two humps, one on top of the woolly mammoth's head and one above its front shoulders, stored fat that the mammoth could use as a reserve when food was hard to find.

The mammoth's tusks were actually front biting teeth.

small compared to those of today's elephants. Large ears make sense in hot climates because they help cool an elephant's blood much as a radiator cools a car. But in the arctic cold, less skin surface meant saving body heat.

With its long, curving tusks, a *bull* mammoth must have been a fearful sight to *prehistoric* hunters. The tusks were in fact huge *incisors* (front biting teeth). They were made of a hard, smooth material called ivory. It is the same material that lies beneath the enamel of your own teeth. The tusks averaged 10 to 12 feet in length. A few have been found that measured up to 16 feet. The tusks grew down and out from the upper jaw before curving back toward each other.

The mammoth's tusks were good weapons, but they were even more important at feeding time. When snow covered the ground the bulls plowed the drifts aside with their tusks. Then the entire herd moved in to graze on half-frozen grasses.

The Mammoth's Trunk

Scientists who study dinosaurs have a hard job. When they try to imagine what a brontosaurus looked like, they have only the bones for clues. The woolly mammoth is just as *extinct* as the dinosaur, but there's no need to guess how it looked. A number of woolly mammoths have been found in nature's "deep freeze"–buried in Siberian or Alaskan ice. For this reason naturalists know more about the mammoth than they do about most extinct animals.

The key to the woolly mammoth's survival was its long, hairy trunk. This extra-long snout was much more than a nose. Along with squirting water and gathering food the trunk could reach and grasp like an arm and hand. The Asiatic elephant has a fingerlike lobe on the end of its trunk, which lets it grasp small objects. The woolly mam-

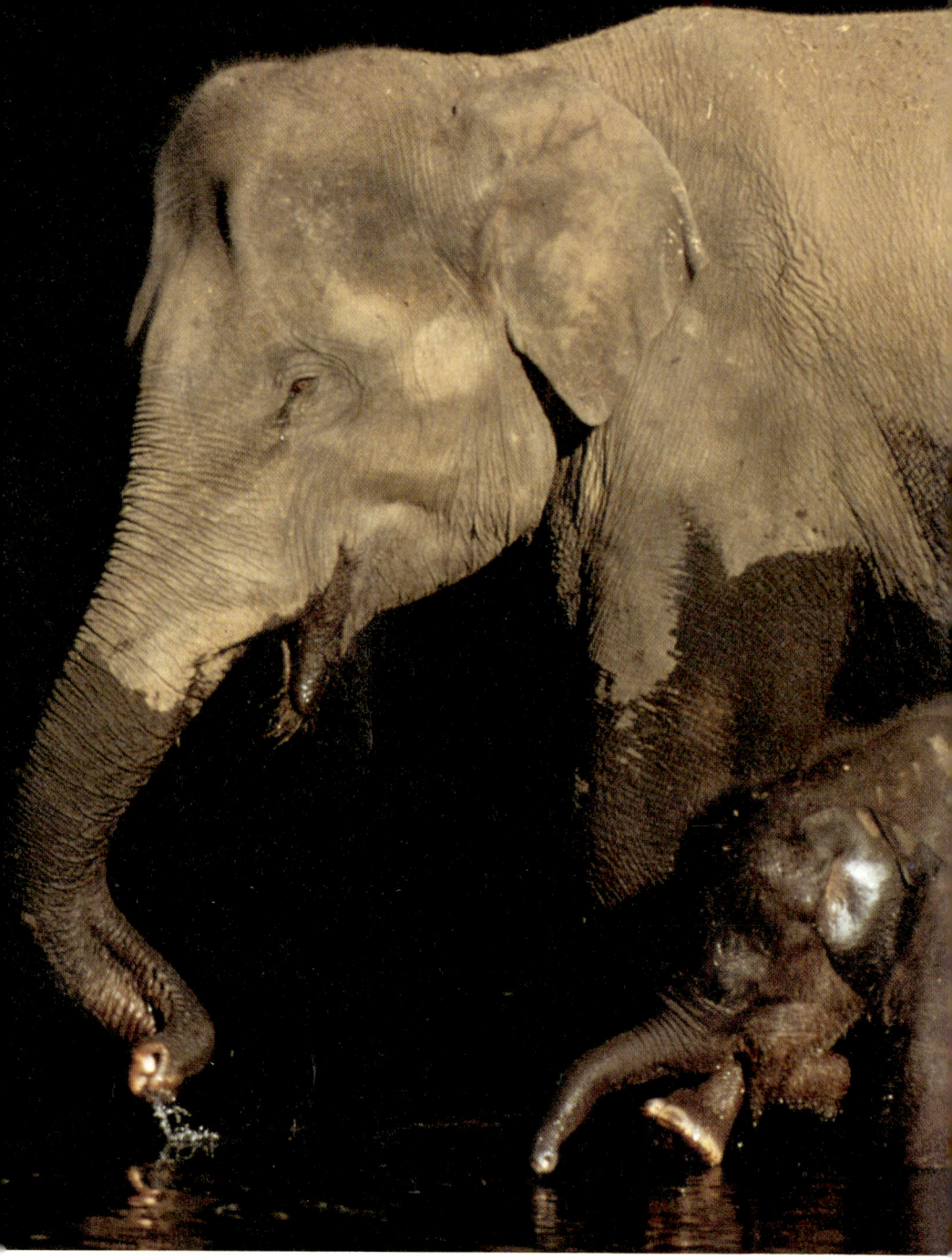

The Asiatic elephant can grab small objects with the tip of its trunk. This cow and her calf are using their trunks as straws.

moth had two such "fingers" at the end of its trunk. One was located above the nostrils, and one below. The mammoth's touch was delicate enough to pick up a bird's egg—and strong enough to move a heavy tree trunk.

The mammoth's trunk was needed at feeding time. The long trunk swept across the ground finding food by scent and by touch. Next, the mammoth curled its trunk around a large bunch of grass and tore it loose. It shaped the grass into a bite-size bundle and stuffed the food into its mouth. After eating, the mammoth found a water hole and sucked water up into its trunk. Then the trunk curled and sprayed the water into the mammoth's open mouth.

An adult mammoth had only four teeth, two in each jaw. The large, block-shaped teeth were made of hard enamel plates held together by layers of cement. As the soft cement wore away, the surface of each tooth became ridged like a file. Without these ridges the woolly mammoth couldn't have chewed the tough prairie grasses and herbs that it preferred for food. In time the teeth wore out, but new teeth were waiting to take their place. Each tooth was replaced five times during a mammoth's full lifetime.

If they were alive today, woolly mammoths would be called *pachyderms*. That's a Greek word that describes thick-skinned animals such as elephants and rhinoceroses. On its back and sides a mammoth's skin was at least an inch thick. Their skin hung in loose folds so they could twist and turn more easily. In addition to their thick skins, woolly mammoths had a heavy layer of fat under their skins.

When a mammoth's tooth wore down, a new one was always waiting to take its place.

Because modern elephants lack this fat layer, they cannot exist for long in freezing temperatures.

With their size and thick skin for protection, the mammoths didn't need sharp senses. Their small, long-lashed eyes had poor distance vision. Because they couldn't turn their heads, mammoths turned their bodies to look to the left or right. With their weak eyes the woolly mammoths depended on their keen sense of smell to warn of danger. By raising their trunks high to sniff the air, the animals knew at once if wolves were hiding upwind.

Like most *herbivores*, or plant eaters, woolly mammoths traveled in herds. As the herd moved across the plains, the animals kept in touch with trumpet calls and deep, rumbling sounds. These shaggy creatures were well adapted to their cold northern habitat.

A Hungry Giant

During the ice ages herds of woolly mammoths ranged across much of the Northern Hemisphere. This was a time when huge rivers of ice–*glaciers*–moved slowly across the land. Because much of the world's water was frozen in glaciers, the sea level dropped. Land bridges linked Asia to North America and the British Isles to Europe. The mammoths migrated. Mammoth bones are found in Britain, northern Europe, Siberia, Alaska, Canada, the United States, and Mexico.

The remains of hundreds of woolly mammoths have been found in a single area. This tells naturalists that the mammoths moved in large herds. Each herd occupied a range that covered many square miles. In the spring the herds moved northward. They grazed on the new growth that covered the plains. Winter weather sent the herds southward in their constant search for food.

A 10,000-pound herbivore needs a lot of food. Each full-sized woolly mammoth could eat about 600 pounds of plants each day. The stomach contents of frozen mammoths told scientists what they ate. Woolly mammoths

Much like elephants today, mammoths depended on huge quantities of grasses and plant life for their survival. A full-sized woolly mammoth could eat 600 pounds of food a day.

lived on prairie grasses, sedges, mosses, leaves, and alpine plants. But their digestive systems could turn only about half of what they ate into energy. That's why mammoths grazed for up to 16 hours a day. A herd of hungry mammoths quickly stripped an area of its edible plants. Day by day, the herd moved onward, driven by the need for new grazing land.

As the heavy animals roamed the grasslands they sometimes trampled the earth into sunken trails. These "mammoth trails" are most often found near water holes and *salt licks*. Water was vital to the mammoths. These animals could drink up to 40 gallons each day. A good water hole was also useful for bathing. During the dry months the bulls dug water holes with their tusks in muddy streambeds.

The woolly mammoth was not a fast-moving animal. A typical herd traveled at a slow six miles per hour. Their progress was often slowed while members of the herd stopped to graze. Like a pacing horse, the mammoth's walking gait began with both left legs swinging forward, followed by the two right legs. An attack by a sabertooth cat sent the woolly mammoth into a lumbering trot. For brief bursts, a charging bull could reach 18 miles per hour. Because of its weight and the way its legs were jointed, the mammoth wasn't able to jump. If the herd wouldn't step across a gulley, it had to detour around it.

The woolly mammoth survived in Siberia long after it became extinct in North America and Europe. Most people think of Siberia as a cold and lifeless land, but that has not always been true. Between the ice ages, and after the last one, a warmer climate created ideal grazing lands there. The Siberian *tundra* (rolling grasslands) grew sedges, wild thyme, crowsfoot, Alpine poppy, and many grasses. This vast area is three-fourths the size of the United States.

The Birth of a Woolly Mammoth

No modern human being has seen a live woolly mammoth, so when scientists try to reconstruct the mammoth's life cycle, they depend on careful detective work. The clues they use come from fossil bones and tusks, frozen bodies, and paintings left by stone age hunters. These clues give us a good picture of the woolly mammoth. Careful study of the animal's blood, teeth, and internal organs adds further information.

The woolly mammoth's family tree provides another important clue. Although the mammoth wasn't an elephant, it was closely related to the Asiatic elephant. This fact leads to a useful conclusion: The woolly mammoth's behavior was probably similar to the modern elephant's. By using elephants as a model, we can imagine the life of a woolly mammoth with some accuracy.

Go back in time some 10,000 years. You're standing on a low hill overlooking the Siberian tundra. Below you a small herd of woolly mammoths is grazing. It's late spring and the northern days are long and warm. As you watch, a *cow* wanders away from the main herd and hides in a brush-choked ravine. You can see that she will soon give birth to a *calf*.

The calf is born during the night. You'd like to move closer, but a watchful female mammoth is standing guard. When the sun rises, you see the newborn calf. It stands about three feet tall on its wobbly legs. If you could push it onto a scale it would weigh around 220 pounds. The calf's wrinkled skin is covered by a coat of fine reddish brown hair. It will shed this birth hair when it grows its heavy adult coat.

The calf pushes under its mother's belly and begins to

Because the woolly mammoth was closely related to the Asiatic elephant, scientists study the habits of the Asiatic elephant to learn more about the mammoth.

nurse. Within a few days it will be drinking almost three gallons of milk each day. The calf can digest the tall Siberian grasses, but it can't chew them yet. The two cows know how to solve this problem. They chew up bite-size wads of grass and feed them to the calf.

Within a few days the calf is strong enough to keep up with the herd. Several times a day the mother kneels to let the calf nurse. If she's not close by, the calf wanders over and nurses from one of the other cows. The herd is led by an older cow who knows where to find the best grasses and water holes. Once a week she leads them to an outcropping of salt-bearing rocks. The mammoths need the salt to properly digest their food.

As you follow the herd it comes to the edge of a river. The mammoths swim across, using their trunks like a skin diver's snorkel. The calves hold tight to their mothers' tails. On the far bank, the male calves begin to play-fight. They butt foreheads and hook with their small milk tusks. Like baby teeth, the milk tusks will be replaced by adult tusks when the calves are older. When they reach maturity (age 12 to 16), the bulls will be much larger than the cows.

Play-fighting prepares the calves for more serious battles. When they're older, they'll have to fight off the predators that prey on newborn calves and old, sick adults. In addition, they'll have to fight for mates. Only a few woolly mammoths live out their full life spans. Some will die of disease. A few will be trapped in muddy bogs or will fall into crevices in the ice. Their greatest danger, however, comes from human hunters.

Did Stone Age People Hunt the Woolly Mammoth?

The last 600,000 years of the earth's history have been marked by several ice ages. Each time the climate turned

This painting shows an area of Alaska where woolly mammoths lived with many other mammals—including bears, wolverines, and yaks—12,000 years ago.

cold huge arctic glaciers crept southward to cover the land. During those periods, many cold-loving mammals lived in the Northern Hemisphere. The woolly rhinoceros, the musk ox, the cave bear, and the woolly mammoth were only a few of them.

Traces of humans have been found in northern Europe, Asia, and North America. Burial sites, caves, and ancient fires mark the camps of the *Stone Age* peoples. These discoveries, which are only a few hundred years old, once set off a major debate. Did the cave dwellers live at the same time as the woolly mammoth?

Scientists found evidence of Stone Age humans mixed with those of ice age animals. In addition to stone tools they found small carvings made of ivory. From these they concluded that Stone Age humans did live at the same time as the woolly mammoth. The argument didn't end there, however. Other scientists said that humans couldn't have lived in northern lands during the ice ages. The cold was too great, they claimed, and the mammoth was too large to be hunted with stone weapons. Maybe Stone Age artists were carving tusks they'd picked up from long-dead mammoths.

Other discoveries raised further questions. Near a village in Czechoslovakia farmers uncovered a hill full of mammoth fossils. When scientists arrived on the scene, they found human bones and tools mixed in as well. Could Stone Age hunters have killed so many mammoths? Was the site a "mammoth graveyard" where old and sick mammoths came to die? A great storm may have trapped the mammoths in a ravine, where they were buried in a mudslide. Or human hunters armed with torches may have driven the mammoths off a cliff.

In the early 1900s, the human-mammoth question finally was answered. People found more carvings and cave paintings of woolly mammoths. Only hunters who had seen living mammoths could have made these drawings. From long trunks to high, fatty humps, the ancient artists pictured the mammoths in exact detail. Other scenes showed hunters attacking mammoths with lances and arrows. The

This drawing is based on a description of one of the woolly mammoths found frozen in ice and shipped to the Academy of Sciences in St. Petersburg, Russia.

experts said the paintings and carvings were a type of hunting magic. Capturing the mammoth in a drawing, the cave dwellers believed, would bring them success in the actual hunt.

How did Stone Age hunters kill such huge animals? For one thing, the woolly mammoth was large, but it wasn't savage. It was not afraid of humans. It probably didn't run when hunters came near.

The hunters' first task was to creep close to a grazing mammoth. Then, on a signal, they ran forward and plunged lances into the mammoth's underside. Used with skill, the

Stone Age hunters had to get close to a mammoth in order to plunge their swords and lances into the animal's underside.

hunters' lances would strike a vital spot and the beast would die. A number of mammoth fossils have been found with spear points buried deep in the great ribs. Also, the hunters probably used the animals' fear of fire to drive them into traps. Hunting the woolly mammoth was dangerous, but it wasn't impossible.

The Mystery of the Mammoth's Extinction

Until the mid-1800s, most people rejected the idea that animals could become extinct. After all, they argued, God would not have created a species that wasn't meant to be on the earth forever. When the woolly mammoth's bones came to light, they were said to belong to a race of giant humans.

Charles Darwin's theory of *evolution* finally helped people understand that animals do change. Darwin believed nature is constantly testing every species. In any group of animals some will be better able to survive than others. So when the climate turned colder, some mammoths froze to death. The mammoths with the warmest coats lived and gave birth to long-haired calves. After many years, only mammoths with warm, shaggy coats were left.

Thanks in part to Darwin, people finally accepted the fact that the strange bones belonged to an elephantlike animal. Were any woolly mammoths still alive? If not, why did they die out?

Most scientists now believe the woolly mammoth disappeared from North America and Europe at least 10,000 years ago. After that, the species may have lived on in Siberia for another 4,000 years. As late as 1920, however, a Russian hunter claimed to have seen "elephant tracks" in the snow of northern Siberia. The hunter followed the tracks and caught a glimpse of a "huge elephant with big white tusks" and long reddish hair. Naturalists don't believe the story. They say it is a folktale, similar to the legends of Bigfoot or the Abominable Snowman.

Despite the hunter's story, the woolly mammoth is almost certainly extinct. One of the earliest theories about the disappearance was the Great Flood Theory. Many religions tell stories of a great flood that once covered the entire earth. The only animals that survived were those that floated to safety on a huge boat. According to this theory, the woolly mammoth missed the boat. There's no evidence, however, that the mammoth's northern habitat was ever covered by a great flood.

The Cold Wave Theory imagines a different disaster. A series of volcanic eruptions might have filled the air with thick clouds of dust. By cutting off much of the sunlight the dust would have lowered temperatures all around the world. The sudden cold, lasting for a year or more, could have destroyed the mammoth's food supply. A similar effect could have been caused by a giant meteor hitting the earth.

Scientists have many theories about how the woolly mammoth became extinct. One theory said cold temperatures that lasted more than a year cut off the mammoths' food supply, and the animals died of starvation.

As with the flood, there's no evidence of such a disaster during the time the mammoth disappeared.

The Giantism Theory says woolly mammoths grew too large to survive. Any change in the climate that reduced the food supply would cause large animals to die out. The theory sounds good until someone points out that other elephant-size animals survived quite well. Warmer or colder temperatures could have destroyed the food supply in one region. Mammoth herds, however, were capable of traveling great distances to find good grazing.

The Blitzkrieg Theory is perhaps the best. Twenty thousand years ago, scientists say, mammoths lost their ability to adapt to change. It was a time when warmer weather was replacing the grasslands with thick forests. At the same time, Stone Age hunters were killing mammoths by the thousands. With food scarce, the herds couldn't breed fast enough to replace their losses. Finally, only frozen bodies and buried bones were left to tell the story of the woolly mammoth.

The Mystery of the Giant Bones

Five hundred years ago the people of Europe were puzzled by a great mystery. While building a church in southern France, workers uncovered some huge bones. No one had ever seen an animal big enough to produce such bones.

"Ah," some people said, "these are the bones of dragons." Other experts studied the fossils and decided that they were the bones of giants. After all, the Bible says that giants once lived on the earth.

People studied the bones and tried to guess the size of these giants. Judging by the length of a thighbone, one doctor declared that they must have been 20 feet tall. "The head alone is as large as a round table, the arms as thick as the body of a man," another writer reported. In 1613, a French doctor put some mammoth bones on display. He said they belonged to a dead German king named Teutobochus. Crowds came and marveled at the bones of the mighty king.

When tusks were found, they created another problem. Giants didn't have tusks, did they? The "experts" found another answer. "These are the horns of the lost unicorn," they said. "Giant bones" and "unicorn horns" became very popular. People hung them over the doors of churches and displayed them in city halls.

Scientists were beginning to have their doubts. After all, the fossils didn't look like human bones. The "arms" were more like the bones of four-legged animals. The skulls were the wrong sizes and shapes. In fact, when the bones were put together a nonhuman shape emerged. Jean Riolan, another French doctor, said the bones of Teutobochus were really those of an elephant. People laughed at him. Everyone knew that tropical animals couldn't live in the cold European climate.

The debate went on. Some suggested that the "bones"

When the first mammoth bones were discovered, people thought they were the bones of a giant. Later, scientists realized they belonged to a four-legged animal.

weren't really bones at all. "They're really rocks, shaped like bones," these skeptics said. Another theory declared that the bones were the remains of war elephants. This idea was based on the fact that Hannibal of Carthage had used elephants in his wars against Rome. A related theory claimed that the bones came from elephants that traveled with circuses!

New finds were being made all the time. In 1644, a skeleton with some of the flesh still attached was found in Austria. The bones of other animals, such as hippopotamuses, were also being dug up. In North America, similar

35

discoveries had been made. In Mexico, the Spanish conquerors found thighbones as tall as a man. In 1705, more bones and teeth were found in New York. One tooth weighed nearly five pounds.

By now, most of the old theories had been thrown out. If the bones didn't come from giants or unicorns or elephants, however, where did they come from? An English explorer named Josias Logan found an important clue in 1611. Some Siberian natives sold him a piece of ivory they had found near their village. Logan was surprised to find an "elephant tusk" in the frozen north. If Siberia could provide such tusks, he felt there was more to be learned about these finds.

Logan was right. Siberia was the key to solving the mystery of the giant bones.

Mammoths in the Ice

While Europe wrestled with the mystery of the giant bones, Siberian natives were selling mammoth tusks. Most of the trade was with China. The Chinese believed the tusks came from giant moles that never left their underground burrows. Why hadn't anyone ever seen the moles? Well, the story said, the moles died as soon as they ventured into the sunlight.

Other reports added to the legend. In 1685, a French priest reported that the Siberians called the ivory-bearing animal the Behemot. The priest believed the Behemot still lived in some Siberian rivers. A few years later a Dutch diplomat added to the Chinese story. The creature was really a giant rat called a Mammut, he said. Mammuts died, it was said, when floods forced them into the open air. This seemed to explain why mammoth remains were found usually after the spring thaw.

In the late 1700s, a better theory appeared. Working from bones found in Europe, Johann Blumenbach declared that the long-dead creatures were related to elephants. That theory raised a new question. Could a tropical species such as the elephant have lived in a northern climate? Most people thought it was impossible. Winter temperatures of 50 degrees below zero were common in Siberia. Only a few scientists guessed that the Siberian climate had once been much warmer.

In 1723, Siberia produced the next breakthrough. A whole woolly mammoth was found in the melting ice. Wolves had eaten most of the body, but a large piece of fur-covered skin was recovered. Because the skin seemed fresh, people thought the mammoths still lived in the area. News of the find was slow to reach Europe, however. Years later the government ordered the natives to search for more mammoth remains. A single hunter brought in over 150 tusks! A new ivory rush began. Thousands of mammoths were found, and the natives sold 50,000 pounds of ivory each year.

Until the 1800s, no scientist had ever seen a newly unearthed mammoth. When natives found a frozen mammoth they left it alone. They believed that creatures from

Few woolly mammoth calves lived out their full life span. Some died of disease. Others fell into tar pits, crevices, or bogs. Still others were brought down by the spears of hunters.

the underworld would be angry if anyone disturbed the frozen mammoth. After the bones and tusks were scattered, however, it was all right to harvest them. Finally, in 1805, word of a thawed mammoth carcass reached a scientist named Mikhail Adams. Adams worked at Russia's Academy of Sciences in St. Petersburg.

When Adams got to the site he found that wolves and sled dogs had fed upon the body. The trunk was missing and someone had already collected the tusks. Even so, the skull was covered with skin. One eye, the brain, and the side lying on the ground were in good shape. The gray skin was covered with thick, reddish brown hair. When Adams cut the hide from the bones, it took ten men to lift it. The hair that fell from the undamaged side weighed 37 pounds. The ankle of the right front leg and the 350-pound head were preserved intact. Adams loaded the remains on dog sleds and shipped them to St. Petersburg.

Experts rebuilt the skeleton for display in the Academy of Sciences museum. All talk of "giant's bones" and "giant rats" was forgotten. The mammoth was clearly a hairy, cold-loving, elephantlike animal. Thanks to Mikhail Adams and the Siberian deep freeze, the fossil record was taking shape.

The Creation of Fossils

Without nature's fossil record scientists would never have solved the mystery of the woolly mammoth. To a *paleontologist* (a scientist who studies fossils), the ancient bones, tusks, and frozen body parts tell a convincing story. A fossil, however, doesn't have to be as big as a mammoth's skull or as complete as a frozen body. If you're lucky, the next rock you break open may reveal the fossil outline of a million-year-old snail.

Only a few dead plants and animals turn into fossils. The soft tissues of living things usually decay and disappear after they die. The harder parts, such as an insect's shell or a mammoth's backbone, are more likely to survive. Paleontologists classify fossils in four categories: petrified fossils, molds and casts, prints, and whole plants and animals.

Petrified fossils. Arizona's famous Petrified Forest is made up of good examples of this type of fossil. Instead of rotting on the surface, these trees were buried under mud or sand. Dissolved minerals slowly replaced each cell of the once-living trunks and turned the wood to stone. In other cases, minerals filled in the small air spaces of buried shells or bones. As the stones formed, they took on the exact shape of the originals.

Molds and casts. Imagine for a moment that a lizard has been buried in the mud of a forest. Soon afterward the mud dries out and becomes rock hard. The lizard decays, but the newly formed rock retains the exact shape of the reptile's body. Later, another material seeps into the mold, hardens, and forms a casting. The casting is an exact copy of the lizard.

Prints. When thin objects are covered by mud or dirt they become trapped just as the lizard did. Later, if the mud turns to rock, a faint print of the decayed leaf or feather may be left behind. You can get the same effect by pressing a fern into a block of clay. When you strip the fern from the clay, you'll leave a "fossil print" behind.

Whole plants and animals. Whole plants and animals rarely become fossils. When a woolly mammoth was totally encased in ice, the skin and flesh were preserved. Except for a baby mammoth discovered in Alaska, all the whole fossils of this mighty animal have been found in Siberia. Paleontologists guess that most mammoths were trapped when they stepped on what looked like a safe snowfield.

When a woolly mammoth crossed a snowfield, its weight could have broken through the thin crust. The animal may have then been trapped in a deep crevice.

Their great weight broke through the thin crust and they fell into deep crevices or icy rivers. Unable to free themselves, they died in what became a natural deep freeze.

In 1900, for example, Russian scientists recovered the body of a woolly mammoth in northeastern Siberia. A landslide had exposed the animal, which was frozen into the side of a cliff. When they examined the body, scientists found that the mammoth hadn't digested its last meal. Locked in the arctic cold for all those years, the heart and liver, brain, eyes, tongue, and muscles were still intact. Thanks to the fossil record, the story of the woolly mammoth was finally completed.

Scientists Recreate a Woolly Mammoth

This story begins 50,000 years ago. Somewhere in Europe, a stream flows across a grassy plain. Along its banks, woolly mammoths are grazing. Spring brings heavy rains, and the stream overflows. A young mammoth walks across muddy fields to drink. Suddenly, it slips and falls into the cold water. Unable to regain its footing, the animal tumbles deep into the stream. Caught between two boulders, it drowns.

As the dead mammoth decays, the body breaks up. Carried downstream by the current, the bones pile up at a sharp bend. Year by year they're buried more deeply under new layers of mud. A thousand years later the stream dries up. The bones remain hidden far below the surface.

The time now shifts to the present. A city has grown up on the ancient plain. Workers move in with heavy equipment to dig the foundations for a new building. A bulldozer blade uncovers the mammoth's fossilized bones. Work stops while the workers call the local museum and ask for an expert.

The scientist arrives with a truckload of student volunteers. They have a well-prepared plan for making the *dig*. First, they map the area and record the location of each find. Careful hands use fine brushes to clean the dirt off the bones, many of which have broken into hundreds of pieces. Each bone, large and small, is covered with plaster for its trip to the museum.

Back at the museum the bones are spread out on large tables. The plaster is removed, and a student measures each piece and gives it a number. Then the task of fitting the pieces together begins. Using a textbook, the paleontologist identifies each of the mammoth's nearly 300 bones. After a bone is complete, a coating of glue is applied to hold it together. Other students make patches to fill in missing pieces. Once the patches are approved, they are stained to match the original bones.

When the bones have been preserved, work begins on the museum display. The team calls in artists and engineers to help them prepare a *diorama,* or exhibit. The artists design a background that recreates a mammoth's habitat. Along with a distant herd of mammoths, they paint in the plants

Scientists spend many months piecing together bones of extinct animals for research and for exhibits in museums.

and animals that also lived on the grasslands. Meanwhile, the skeleton is taking shape. Guided by an engineer, students drill holes in the bones. Steel rods inserted in the holes support the 800 pounds of bone. Extra wires support the 50-pound tusks.

As the last bone is put in place, the woolly mammoth's skeleton stands nearly ten feet tall. When spotlights are turned on, the scene looks almost real. The students gaze at the towering skeleton and feel a great sense of pride. Thanks to their efforts, an extinct animal has been given a new life.

What Have We Learned?

Scientists believe that the last woolly mammoth died thousands of years ago. Even so, this extinct animal still has lessons to teach us.

No species is immune from extinction. For a long time, woolly mammoths were able to adjust as the ice ages came and went. With their warm coats and great size, millions of mammoths lived peacefully on the cold tundra. Then something went wrong. The species could no longer adapt to changes in the climate. To make matters worse, Stone Age hunters were killing great numbers of mammoths. Sometimes they killed an animal and took only its heart or liver. Finally, the day came when the hunters returned empty-handed. The mammoth was gone.

Depending on a single way of life can be fatal. The woolly mammoth needed rich grasslands in order to survive. Within a few lifetimes, however, changes in climate turned their grasslands into forests. Forced to migrate, many woolly mammoths weakened and died.

A species can speed its own extinction. When food became scarce woolly mammoths reacted by overgrazing. The animals pulled up plants by the roots and turned the land into desert.

No species is safe when humans decide to exploit it. Although Stone Age people were dwarfed by woolly mammoths, they possessed superior brains. The hunters developed weapons and tactics that allowed them to kill mammoths for their meat and skins. With their small brains, the mammoths never learned to avoid the new danger.

All life on Earth is part of a single system. Some of the most dramatic pictures of recent times were taken from space. The color photos of the earth made people realize that we all share a single planet. The loss of any species, whether it is a mammoth or a moth, makes the entire world poorer.

Will we listen to the woolly mammoth? The lesson can be summed up in a single sentence: Once a species becomes extinct, it is gone forever.

For More Information

For more information about the woolly mammoth, write to:

The George C. Page Museum
5801 Wilshire Boulevard
Los Angeles, CA 90036

Glossary/Index

Bull 16, 23, 26 – an adult male woolly mammoth.
Calf 18, 24, 25, 26, 31, 38 – a young male or female woolly mammoth.
Cow 18, 24, 25, 26 – an adult female woolly mammoth.
Dig 43 – the place where scientists search for fossils and artifacts by digging up the earth.
Diorama 43 – a museum exhibit in which mounted animals are displayed against painted backgrounds.
Evolution 31 – a theory that explains the process by which a species changes over many generations.
Extinct 17, 23, 30, 32, 44, 45, 46 – when all animals of a certain type vanish, as when the last member of that species dies.
Fossils 12, 13, 28, 30, 34, 39, 40, 43 – the remains of ancient living organisms, usually found buried in soil, embedded in rocks, or frozen in ice.
Genus 9 – a certain class of animal or plant.
Glacier 21, 27 – a huge mass of ice and snow that builds up and moves slowly over the land.
Habitat 9, 14, 21, 32 – the place where an animal makes its home.
Herbivores 21 – animals that feed only on plants.
Ice Ages 12, 13, 14, 26, 28, 45 – times when cold weather caused glaciers to form and move southward from the arctic regions.
Incisors 17 – front, biting teeth.

Interbreed 7–to reproduce. The Asiatic and African elephants cannot interbreed.

Ivory 6, 17, 36, 37–the common name for the hard, white substance of which a woolly mammoth's tusks were made.

Naturalist 6, 17, 21, 31–a scientist who studies plants and animals.

Pachyderms 19–certain large, thick-skinned hoofed animals such as elephants, rhinoceroses, and hippopotamuses.

Paleontologist 39, 40–a scientist who studies fossils.

Predators 12, 26–animals that live by killing other animals.

Prehistoric 16–before recorded history.

Salt lick 22–a place where animals go to lick the salt they find in rocks or in the soil.

Species 6, 7, 9, 11, 31, 45, 46–a single kind of plant or animal.

Stone Age 28, 29, 30, 31, 45–the period in history when humans began to use stone tools.

Trunk 6, 12, 17, 18, 19, 20, 26–the woolly mammoth's strong, flexible, extended snout.

Tundra 23, 24, 45–rolling grasslands.

Tusks 6, 8, 9, 12, 16, 17, 24, 26, 28, 34, 36, 37, 38, 39, 44–extra-long incisor teeth that grew to great length and extended far beyond a mammoth's upper lip.